Reg was about to ring the Burns's doorbell when he heard raised voices inside. He glanced at George, who raised an eyebrow, then went ahead and rang the bell anyway. The door was yanked open.

'Gary Burns?' Reg said.

The man nodded. He was in his mid-thirties, good-looking, fit and confident. 'Er yeah, that's right,' he said.

'PC Hollis and PC Garfield from Sun Hill. Could we have a word?'

Also available in Puffin Books

THE BILL: JUNIOR

The Bill:
Tough Love

Dave Morris

Tough Love original script by
Katharine Way

The Bill series created by Geoff McQueen

PUFFIN BOOKS

PUFFIN BOOKS

Published by the Penguin Group
Penguin Books Ltd, 27 Wrights Lane, London W8 5TZ, England
Penguin Books USA Inc., 375 Hudson Street, New York, New York 10014, USA
Penguin Books Australia Ltd, Ringwood, Victoria, Australia
Penguin Books Canada Ltd, 10 Alcorn Avenue, Toronto, Ontario, Canada M4V 3B2
Penguin Books (NZ) Ltd, 182–190 Wairau Road, Auckland 10, New Zealand

Penguin Books Ltd, Registered Offices: Harmondsworth, Middlesex, England

First published 1997
1 3 5 7 9 10 8 6 4 2

Tough Love produced by Thames Television © 1996
Original script by Katharine Way
All rights reserved

Set in 11.5/16pt Monotype Palatino
Typeset by Rowland Phototypesetting Ltd,
Bury St Edmunds, Suffolk
Printed in England by Clays Ltd, St Ives plc

British Library Cataloguing in Publication Data
A CIP catalogue record for this book is available from the British Library

ISBN 0–140–38516–9

One

THE PERSON WHO'D called the police turned out to be a skinny young black woman in an anorak, leggings and trainers. Her name was Carol Miller and she had been out for her usual early-morning run when, at about seven, she had come across something very odd. As she stopped at the pavilion on Canley Comprehensive's sports ground to get her breath back and check her pulse-rate against her watch, she had become aware of rather disturbing noises coming from inside the building.

She went to meet the police officers as they pulled up outside the pavilion.

'He's in there,' she said as they got out of

1

the Panda car, 'but I can't get the door open.'

PCs Reg Hollis and George Garfield jogged up the stone steps leading to the wooden building. 'All right, love,' George said. 'We'll deal with it.'

Carol Miller followed them. She almost had to run to keep up with them. 'I come this way all the time,' she said. 'I heard shouting, but I thought I was hearing things.'

'OK,' said George. He stood back a little way from the pavilion, a scruffy one-storey building with horizontal wooden panels like a large garden shed and paintwork that failed to hide all the graffiti. The windows were boarded over from the inside but none had been broken. There was no outward sign of any disturbance.

Then he heard a thump and a voice. Probably male, it sounded hoarse but furious. It said: 'Somebody let me out!'

George tried the door, which was painted in black gloss and, like an old school desk, was covered in layers of graffiti and scratched initials. It was locked. He cupped his hands against the wood and called out: 'This is the police. Just hang on in there and I'll get you out.' He listened for a second and then added: 'Are you hurt?'

'I can't move.'

The reply was muffled. George put his ear to the door, but he could not hear any movement immediately inside. The guy probably wasn't directly behind this door, then. George stepped back and aimed a kick at the lock. The door swung open.

Reg approached. He had been looking around at the other side of the pavilion. 'Want a hand, George?'

'Er no,' George replied, 'I think I can manage.'

Reg always offered help, no matter how straightforward the situation. If someone had dialled 999 because a cat was stuck up a tree Reg would offer help. Although he always went by the book, there was something about the way Reg did it that annoyed George. Reg always expected the worst, and the fact that he never failed to turn up at scenes 'just in case' was an example of that. But he was only sticking to the rules, and the fact that he couldn't fault him for that George found doubly irritating.

George entered the building, moving quickly through white-painted wooden rooms which had the peculiar tangy smell of unwashed rugby kit. Here and there a jersey or a mud-caked football boot lay, discarded.

Reg followed him in. Carol Miller peered in through the open door but did not cross the threshold. She was already going to be late for work but, if she had to give this as an excuse, she might as well be in a position to tell everybody as much as possible about it.

In the pavilion changing room a few thin lines of light shone round the edges of the boarded-up windows. It was dark, but not as dark as it had been.

The teenage boy who lay on the hard wooden floor had been in there all night; his hands were roped tightly to a heavy wooden bench and his legs had been tied together like the handles of a skipping rope. He had spent the first few hours yelling for help, and then, as the sounds of traffic from the nearby road dwindled to nothing, he had fallen asleep at last. He had woken several times during the night, on one occasion to find himself slumped over the bench with his hands pinned under him and squashed numb. It felt like waking up and thinking you were lying on joints of chicken, until the feeling started to come back into them with agonizing pins and needles. Then he had tried calling for help again until finally he had fallen into another bone-numbingly uncomfortable sleep.

Now at last people were banging about inside the building. He called out and, turning on to his side, stamped hard on the floor.

A voice outside said: 'George, in here, mate.' Then the door opened and a copper came in. Another copper followed him in. They both looked startled.

'Are you all right?' one of them asked. He came over and began to wrestle with the youngster's bonds.

The youth's voice was high-pitched with fury and hatred. He said, over and over again: 'I'm gonna kill him!'

Two

IN THE CAD room WPC Polly Page answered Reg Hollis's call. 'There's no serious injury, Pol,' he said. 'Just tied up and left. His name's Steve Rourke.'

'Rourke?' Polly said, frowning. 'I know that name.'

Behind Polly, Sergeant Matthew Boyden heard the name and lifted his headset to listen in.

'Says he's been here all night,' Reg was saying. 'No one's reported him missing, have they?'

Polly's eyes ran down the list on the computer screen in front of her. She clicked the mouse button and the screen produced a new display. 'Not as far as we know, Reg.'

'Lives on the Jasmine Allen,' said Reg.

Sergeant Boyden put down his headset and wandered over to Polly's station. 'Well it wouldn't be Steve's dad reporting him missing. He's banged up in Shadwell Prison; three years for GBH.'

Now Polly remembered. 'You mean Ray Rourke?'

'Yeah; that's the geezer,' Sergeant Boyden nodded.

Once Steve Rourke had been freed by the police he became a good deal noisier and cockier. A tallish lad with well-muscled limbs, he had lapsed into surly silence while George had grappled with the butcher's string round his wrists and ankles. There was plenty of it and getting it off the boy had taken quite some time. George's attempts to chat jokingly with him while trying to find out how he had got into such a mess had been met with disgusted grunts. George found this quite amusing in its own way. Here was a lad who thought he was being strong and silent when minutes before he had been hollering for help.

As George escorted him out, Steve grew argumentative and began to show off. He was obviously a boy who lived on nervous energy, and being with him was rather like being with a frisky, rather unpredictable dog that you were not sure was quite harmless. On top of that, Steve was riled because he had been made to look stupid.

'I ain't giving a statement,' he announced, heaving his kit bag over one shoulder.

'Oh yeah?' George grinned. 'And why's that?'

'It was a joke,' Steve declared, rubbing his wrists. 'Look, I don't have to bring charges if I don't want to. It's up to me.'

'Come off it, Steve. Someone ties you up, scares the living daylights . . .'

'I wasn't scared,' Steve said immediately.

'No?' George glared at him. 'Who did it? Your mates?'

Steve looked at George stubbornly. 'No comment, officer.' He said it with a certain amount of relish.

George wasn't in the least put off. 'Well,

what were you doing there anyway?'

'Playing football,' Steve replied.

George looked at him suspiciously. 'Oh, you were there for football practice, yeah?' They had reached the steps leading to the road. George took Steve's arm and guided him down towards the Panda, where Reg was waiting.

Steve said, after a moment: 'Yeah. That's what I was doing.' He shook his arm loose, but he continued to walk with George.

'Steve,' George said, 'when we found you, said, "I'm gonna kill him." So who was it? Someone you know?'

'Look, you can't do this,' Steve said confidently. 'You can't question me, you need an appropriate adult.'

'Just this once we're not arresting you,' George replied impatiently. 'We're trying to help.'

Steve's face screwed up in a sneer. 'I don't need your poxy help. I'll sort it myself.' He walked towards the car.

'I wouldn't do that if I were you,' George said heavily.

'Yeah?' Steve called back. 'And how're you going to stop me?'

Reg, leaning against the Panda, had been listening to the argument as they approached. He shrugged as Steve came towards him. 'Steve,' he said, 'why are you letting them get away with it?'

'I won't,' Steve said evenly. There was no anger in his voice; he just seemed confident he could 'sort' the situation out himself.

Reg went round to the driver's side. George opened the back door on the near side. 'Right, come on. We'll give you a lift home.' He looked at Reg over the roof of the Panda. Reg nodded.

'We can have a little chat on the way,' George went on. 'Your family will want to know that you're safe.'

'They won't give a monkey's,' Steve answered defiantly, but he climbed in.

George shut him in and then went round to the back door on the other side. 'Put your seat belt on, please,' he said as he slid into the seat beside him. Steve sat for a moment without doing anything, but Reg was watching him in the driving mirror and did not start the car. Sulkily Steve put the belt on at last, and Reg drove off.

The Jasmine Allen was a grim estate; flats led off narrow walkways, on most doors were signs that locks had been replaced or new ones added. Many of them looked as if they had been given the same rough treatment as the bashed-up pavilion on the Canley sports ground: a good hard kicking.

Steve walked between Reg and George, directing them past a row of orange doors. He stopped at number 30.

George rang the doorbell. A woman with dyed yellow hair answered, pulling the door open a little way and peering through a tiny gap over a chain. Then she undid the chain and opened the door fully. She was plumpish and was wearing a big maroon jumper over pink leggings, and black ankle-boots. Under the mane of blonde hair the rest of her face was pale, as if waiting for make-up. She seemed only mildly surprised to see her son brought home by the police.

'Mrs Cheryl Rourke?' Reg asked.

Steve grunted and stepped past his mother into the flat.

'Don't tell me what he's done,' Cheryl said to Reg and George. 'I don't want to know.' She followed Steve inside, out of sight of the policemen. Then there was a thump and the sound of swearing from inside the flat. Cheryl came back into the hall and indicated to Reg and George to follow her. Resignedly she picked up a fake-fur jacket from a chair in the lounge and took her keys from the table. 'I suppose you want me down the station.' She said it as a statement, not a question.

'Well, no, Mrs Rourke,' said Reg, 'We haven't arrested Steve for anything. Looks like this time he's been the victim.'

Cheryl looked surprised. 'Yeah?' She sucked in her breath like someone dragging on a cigarette. 'Makes a change.' She put the jacket and the keys back. Meanwhile they could hear Steve bad-temperedly chucking things around in his room.

George got out his notebook.

'Someone tied him up and left him in the

12

pavilion,' Reg said. 'A young lady heard him shouting for help.'

At that moment Steve came into the lounge and picked up Cheryl's jacket, putting his hand in one of the pockets. 'Dozy cow called the filth,' he said out of the corner of his mouth.

Cheryl watched him rummaging in her jacket. 'I'll talk to you in a minute,' she said sharply. Steve drew a small red purse out of the pocket and took a folded five-pound note out of it. When he put the garment down it slid off the chair on to the floor as he put the money in his pocket. His Doc Martens narrowly missed stepping on the jacket as he went into the kitchen. 'Are you listening to me?' Cheryl called after him. Cupboard doors banged in the kitchen.

'Look,' George said, 'we don't know who did this, and Steve's not helping us.'

Cheryl stooped to pick up the jacket. 'Look, it's nothing to do with me,' she said irritably.

'But you're his mum,' George said. 'Didn't you notice that he hadn't been home since yesterday?'

Cheryl took the purse out of the pocket and checked inside it. 'He stays out all night sometimes. I've no idea where he goes.' She raised her voice. 'Never tells me what he's doing, does he?' There was no response from Steve. Cheryl continued more quietly: 'His dad's the only person he listens to.'

'Mrs Rourke,' said Reg, 'do you know anyone who might've wanted to teach Steve a lesson?'

Cheryl put the jacket on the chair again. She laughed bitterly. 'Yeah, half the estate. They come and scream at me.' She shrugged. 'What am I supposed to do?'

'Can you think of any one person?' said Reg.

Cheryl was shaking her head before he had even finished the question. It was a question she was used to answering. 'No, I can't.'

'Perhaps you could have a word with Steve,' Reg suggested. 'He might know something.'

She shrugged helplessly. 'Think he listens to me?' She snorted. 'Not since his dad's been

14

gone. And a right lot of help he was before, in any case.'

They heard the scrape of drawers being opened roughly in another room. Steve shouted something.

Cheryl turned around. 'What?' she called, irritated.

Steve came out into the lounge, bare-chested, and stared at Cheryl fixedly. 'Where's me shirt? I've got to go to school.'

'You've changed your tune,' Cheryl snapped. Steve stomped back out into the hallway and into his bedroom. Cheryl smiled weakly at Reg and George. 'Thanks for bringing him back.'

As they walked away George said: 'If someone leaves him there all night, they mean it. It's not just kids mucking about.' He had to talk to Reg's back as the concrete walkway was too narrow for them to walk side by side. 'Anyway, how would they get hold of the key to lock him in there?'

They came to the stairs. 'Let's drop by Steve's school,' Reg suggested. 'See who else is in the team. Maybe the other kids know something.'

'Yeah, OK.' George clicked his PR and hunched his shoulder to speak into it. 'Sierra Oscar from two one eight.'

WPC Polly Page answered. 'Go ahead, George.'

'Yeah, can you contact the head teacher at Canley Comprehensive, please, Pol? Reg and I need access.'

Three

'MR BILL WYATT?' George said. 'You're the caretaker?'

The man was in his fifties and paunchy, with a straight, bushy moustache and an air of quiet authority. He was in the staffroom, making himself a cup of instant coffee with two spoonfuls of sugar. He had a look of humour in his eyes, and he answered George's question by saying: 'I'm not the caretaker any more; they call us maintenance supervisors now.'

George smiled and handed the man a sheet of paper. 'Do any of these names mean anything to you?'

Wyatt picked up his coffee in one hand and

took the list in the other, holding it at arm's length. He probably wore reading glasses usually.

'Rourke,' he said finally, handing the list back. 'Steve Rourke. Vandal.' He wandered over to a rack of pegs and pulled at one of them experimentally. It seemed to be loose and he wobbled it from side to side. 'Most of the damage round here bears his signature.' He tried the pegs next to it. 'A bully too.'

'Oh yeah?' said Reg, 'who's he bully?'

'Whoever he wants to,' Wyatt replied. He turned back to face Reg and George.

'Well, don't the teachers do anything?' Reg asked.

'Not a lot they can do,' Wyatt said. He smiled. 'They have enough trouble trying to remember the kids' names.'

Reg smiled back. 'And this Steve, is there anyone in particular that he picks on?'

'Mike Burns,' said Wyatt. There was no hesitation in his answer.

'Why him?' Reg wondered.

Wyatt thought for a moment, as though he knew what the problem was but that it was

18

hard to explain. He wasn't one for putting thoughts into words. 'I don't know . . . Something about him . . .' He frowned, then shrugged. 'His face doesn't fit.' He took a sip of coffee, then added: 'His dad coaches the school team – Gary Burns.'

George was surprised. 'What? The famous Gary Burns?'

'The one and only,' Wyatt smiled. 'Retired now.'

'He was a professional, wasn't he?' George said. 'Premier league.'

'No. First division,' Reg interrupted quickly. 'They didn't become the Premier League till 1992. He left the game in 1991, didn't he?'

George nodded along with him. He should have known better than to bring this up. Another annoying thing about Reg was that he was a stickler for detail. This was fine for police work but proved very irritating otherwise. 'Yeah, all right, Reg,' he said quietly.

'I mean, it was . . .' Reg went on.

'Reg!' George yelped. Reg gave him an

offended look but went quiet. George resumed his conversation with Wyatt. 'Now Gary Burns is coaching the school team. That's a bit of a come-down, isn't it?'

Wyatt smirked. 'He's done wonders with them, considering.'

Reg said: 'We need to talk to him. Where can we get his address?'

Wyatt tilted his head, indicating the door. 'The school secretary's office.'

Four

THE BURNS FAMILY lived on one of the new luxury developments that had gone up a few years before, in a small, well-kept house made from pale stone, with cottagey windows and roses round the door. Most of the drives contained small but stylish cars – Fiat Puntos, Vauxhall Tigras and the like – in bold colours or metallic finishes.

Reg was about to ring the Burns's doorbell when he heard raised voices inside. He glanced at George, who raised an eyebrow, then went ahead and rang the bell anyway. The door was yanked open.

'Gary Burns?' Reg said.

The man nodded. He was in his mid-thirties,

good-looking, fit and confident. 'Er yeah, that's right,' he said.

'PC Hollis and PC Garfield from Sun Hill. Could we have a word?'

'Yeah, if it's convenient,' George added.

Burns took a step back. 'Yeah. Yeah, come in.' He turned and walked back into the house, and Reg and George followed, George shutting the front door behind them. Gary showed them into the lounge, a long room running the length of the house with windows at either end. Among the pictures on the walls and the mantelpiece were football photographs, some of them featuring Gary, and other soccer memorabilia was scattered about.

Mr Burns didn't ask them to sit down so they stood as a group in the middle of the room. 'Right then,' he said briskly, 'how can I help you?'

'We understand that you coach at Canley Comprehensive,' Reg began.

'Yeah.' Burns smiled ironically. 'A bunch of delinquents, but there's some good players; a lot of talent.'

'Do you know Steve Rourke at all?' Reg asked.

'Striker,' Burns replied promptly. 'What's he done now?'

A boy in school uniform came in through the other door of the living-room, his shirt loose over his trousers and his tie not yet done up. Facially he looked a lot like Gary Burns, but where the man was taut and muscled, Mike Burns was on the fat side. When he moved it looked as though it cost him a great deal of effort, and he appeared very subdued.

'Mike,' Gary Burns said wearily, 'you're gonna be late.'

Mike stayed where he was, his fingers still round each end of his tie. When he spoke it seemed to take a few goes for him to get his voice going and, when he did, it came out in a whine. 'What's happened?'

Gary stared pointedly at him. 'I'll deal with it, OK?'

Mike Burns didn't move, but he looked at Reg.

Reg said: 'Someone tied Steve Rourke up and locked him in the pavilion overnight after practice. We just wondered if you knew anything.'

Mike Burns's expression knotted with anxiety. 'Is he all right?' he said hoarsely.

'Yeah, he's fine,' Reg nodded. 'There's no harm done, we took him home. You do know him, then?'

'Yeah he's –' Mike seemed thrown by the question '– he's in my class.'

Gary Burns's voice cut through almost before Mike had finished speaking. 'You getting ready or what?'

Mike looked at him uncertainly, then at George and Reg; but finally he turned and went out into the hall. Reg watched him go, thinking hard. Something didn't seem right.

Gary Burns turned back to George and Reg. 'If, er – if Steve Rourke's OK, then what are you worried about?' He smiled.

'Oh, we've got a few more enquiries to make,' George said apologetically. 'What time did the practice finish?'

'Six,' Gary said. He shrugged. 'We're out of there by seven.'

'Right.' George nodded.

Reg was looking in the direction Mike had gone. 'Mr Burns,' he said, 'I'd like to have a word with your son, if it's all right with you.'

'Mike won't know anything,' Gary said impatiently. 'He wasn't even there.'

Reg smiled. 'Yeah, well I'd still like to talk to him.' He moved away into the hall after Mike.

George watched Gary Burns as Reg left the room. He thought the man looked a little uneasy.

George tried to get his attention back. On a shelf next to the hi-fi was a cluster of framed headlines from tabloid newspapers: 'Burns roasts Utd defence' – 'Hat-trick!!!' – 'The scorcher'. There was also a photo of Gary looking triumphant.

'Y'know,' George said, 'I reckon I remember that game. You scored in injury time and then it went on to penalties, yeah?' It was obvious he was making conversation but as long as he kept him talking, so what?

'Yeah, that's right,' Gary replied. He couldn't hide the note of pleasure that came into his voice; clearly he liked nothing better than to be asked about his days as a professional footballer. But he also kept glancing towards the door.

'You went to France, didn't you, after that?' Having started this line of questioning, George was racking his brains to continue it.

'No; Italy,' Gary Burns replied.

George nodded. 'Must've been nice.'

A frown appeared on Gary's forehead. 'My wife thought so,' he replied tartly. 'Mike and I came back after six months and she stayed on.'

'Oh,' George said, embarrassed. 'I'm sorry.'

Gary Burns gave a smile that wasn't entirely unhappy. He made a sweeping motion with his hand. 'I don't display all the newspaper cuttings about that,' he said shortly.

There was something boastful in the way Gary said it: as if he was almost proud of the newspaper gossip instead of disgusted by it. George nodded. He decided he was getting well out of his depth and that he had better go back to asking straightforward questions.

26

'So when exactly did you last see Steve Rourke?'

Gary sounded casual. 'In the pavilion, getting changed. I have a word with them after the session.'

'Right, and then what happens? Do you lock up?'

Gary shook his head. 'No, no. I don't have any keys. Someone locks up after me. Not that there's anything there to steal.'

Reg found Mike upstairs in his bedroom. The boy was reaching for his blazer, and he had to step over a bike that occupied most of the floor in order to reach the wardrobe. The bike looked new but its front wheel had a large kink in it, so that it was almost kidney-shaped. Beside it on the floor was a pair of pliers, but a simple toolkit wasn't going to sort out that kind of damage.

'What happened to your bike?' Reg asked.

'I'm mending it,' said Mike, buttoning up his blazer and not looking at Reg.

'You don't get many mountain bikes in Sun Hill,' Reg said brightly, but the joke fell flat.

Mike stared at him unhappily. 'What d'you want?'

Reg tried a different angle. 'How d'you find school?'

'Boring,' Mike said immediately. 'Why?'

Reg looked sympathetic. 'D'you get on, you know, with the other kids?'

Mike sat on the bed and looked at him suspiciously. 'What are you getting at?'

Reg suspected that he was getting warm.

They heard someone come half-way up the stairs. Then Gary called out: 'Mike! Have you finished? We're running late as it is.'

Reg heard Mike groan quietly. But the boy did not move.

'Mike,' Gary called again, 'are you ready?'

'I'm not going to school,' Mike replied.

Gary called out briskly, 'Well, you're not staying here, I can tell you that for free.'

Reg left Mike to it. He met George on the stairs and they exchanged a glance.

There was no more to ask Gary, so George and Reg went back to the Panda.

George sighed. 'Look,' he said, unlocking

the car, 'if Steve doesn't want to press charges, there's not a lot we can do.'

'Yeah,' Reg replied, but he seemed dissatisfied. 'I'd just like to talk to Mike some more.'

'What for?' George got into the driver's seat.

Mike Burns walked out of the gate and crossed the road. He seemed completely wrapped up in his thoughts.

Reg climbed in on the passenger side. 'Well, he seemed really upset earlier on, when he heard what happened.' George started the engine and pulled out into the road. 'If you ask me, he's scared stiff.'

'Yeah.' George sighed and took his foot off the accelerator. 'I suppose it's worth a try.'

Mike had gone only a few yards. They drove slowly up to him and Reg wound down the window. 'Mike,' he called out, 'd'you want a lift?'

Mike looked up at the mention of his name. He seemed nervous, then replied: 'I'm – I'm late for school.' He seemed to shrink away from the car.

'Yeah, yeah,' Reg nodded. 'Canley Comprehensive.' The Panda had stopped. 'We're going that way.' He reached behind him and opened the nearside back door. 'Hop in.'

A little hesitantly Mike got into the back seat and put on his seat belt. George drove off. The PRs crackled.

Mike watched Reg and George suspiciously in the mirror. 'So, d'you give lifts to people, then?' he asked in a bolshy tone.

'Not officially, no,' George replied. At the junction with the main road he brought the Panda smoothly to a halt at a red light.

Reg smiled. 'You seemed a bit upset earlier on. Anything wrong?'

'No,' Mike snapped emphatically. 'Why?'

'Just wondered.' Reg shrugged and looked out of the window.

'What're you getting at?' Mike demanded.

George pulled out of the junction. 'Look,' he said. 'You know Steve Rourke. D'you know who would've done that to him?'

'That's why you gave me a lift,' Mike said immediately, 'so you can question me unofficially.' His voice rose easily as he became upset.

'All right,' George said. 'Calm down.'

They were nearly at the school. Kids in Canley Comprehensive uniform were walking along the road, carrying large bags and chatting and laughing.

'Let me out,' Mike insisted.

'We'll just take you up to that gate,' said George calmly, going round a small roundabout.

Mike's voice rose even more. He was panicking. 'No, here!' he shouted.

'All right,' said Reg, with a glance at George. George moved the Panda over to the side of the road.

Mike had got his seat belt off and was pushing the door open before the car had fully stopped. He slammed the door behind him and ran away down the road.

George started the Panda again slowly and they watched the boy go up the school steps through a crowd of other kids. He kept his head well down, and none of them seemed to say hello to him. Further up the steps was a smaller group, who began to jeer when they saw Mike approaching.

31

It was Reg who recognized the ringleader. 'Talk of the devil,' he muttered.

With heavy-handed mock politeness Steve Rourke was opening the gate at the top of the steps so as to let Mike Burns through. Mike hesitated then walked through, looking very tense and not glancing to either side.

'There's something going on,' Reg announced. He continued looking out of the window long after George had stopped.

George put the Panda in gear and pulled out. 'It's just kids winding each other up. We're only gonna make it worse for him. We'd better go.'

Five

'IT WAS NOTHING at all like a vendetta if you ask me,' said PC Tony Stamp. 'It was more like an initiation ceremony.'

Four officers were sitting round a table in the Sun Hill canteen, where Steve Rourke's night in the pavilion was the gossip of the moment.

Tony's eyes were like currants in the middle of a bun. They became even smaller when he smiled. 'We used to have this at my school. Two of the big lads stuck your head down the toilet for about thirty seconds, unless you hollered – and then it was a minute.' He gave a big grin.

'Oh, that explains a lot about you, Tony,'

33

said George drily. He stirred sugar into a cup of coffee.

'It's normal, isn't it?' Tony said. 'It doesn't mean anything. All kids are like that.'

'Speak for yourself,' murmured Polly Page, who was sitting next to him. Everyone laughed.

George sighed. 'Yeah, well some kids just get picked on, and Mike Burns is one of them. He might as well walk round with a sign saying "Hit Me".'

Reg was dipping a spoon into a cup, prodding at a herbal tea-bag to persuade it to give out a little more flavour. He looked up. 'I was bullied at school,' he said casually.

'No, Reg,' Polly cooed. 'Really?'

There was more laughter, but Reg stayed quiet.

'I wonder why,' Tony said quietly.

'You know what it's like,' Reg went on with perfect seriousness. 'Some kids . . . they don't have to actually do anything to you, they just put the fear of God into you.' He lifted the herbal tea-bag out and put it carefully in a used cup. 'I remember one bloke . . .'

Tony was already looking at his watch. He got up. 'Some other time, Reg,' he said with a tight smile. He put his hat on and picked up his tea. The others followed suit, getting up and leaving.

WPC Debbie Keane was on duty at the front desk at half-past eleven when Gary Burns strode in. Something about the way he walked suggested that he was upset.

'Can I help you, sir?' Debbie Keane said calmly.

'Yeah I hope so, love,' Gary replied. He ran a hand through his untidy hair. 'I want a word with your inspector. My name is Gary Burns.' He smiled at her expectantly.

His manner suggested a mixture of agitation and self-satisfaction, like a star player waiting for the whistle to start the game. Debbie, of course, knew that a star player was exactly what he was, but she remained aloof and professional. 'Right, sir,' she said smoothly. 'Could you tell me what it's about?'

Gary took a deep breath. 'My son's gone missing. His name's Mike Burns. He's fifteen.'

The WPC remained calm. 'He's not at school?' she asked.

Gary shot back, 'If he was, I wouldn't be here. Look, can I talk to someone in charge, please?'

Debbie reached under the desk and brought out a form and a pen. 'I need some details first,' she said.

Gary paused and looked around. Debbie guessed he was wondering how far he could push his demand to see the inspector. She waited patiently with her pen poised over the form.

Eventually he said: 'At a quarter to ten, Mike's school rang me at work, telling me he was being sent home, ill. So I went home. He never turned up.'

Debbie was writing. She looked up. 'So the school don't know where he is?'

Gary didn't like her tone. The way she asked suggested that he hadn't thought to ask the school. 'No one does,' he retorted. 'It's a ten-minute walk home.' Then he forced his voice to sound a little calmer. 'They don't have any idea where he's gone.'

'Maybe he's bunking off school,' Debbie said. 'A lot of kids do that –'

Gary could have predicted that she would say that. Why did the police talk down to you as if they knew it all? Mike wasn't a juvenile delinquent, he was an authority-fearing kid. 'Mike doesn't,' he interrupted.

Debbie raised an eyebrow. 'Are you sure?'

'Positive,' he said, and smiled.

Debbie wrote something on the form, then she looked up. 'Mr Burns, is there any reason why he'd be upset?'

Gary shrugged. 'Can't think of anything.'

'Well, does your wife –'

'We're divorced,' Gary announced.

Debbie took a breath. 'Well, is there any way Mike could have gone to see her, then?'

Gary smiled before he answered. 'Not really, no. She's in Hong Kong.' He enjoyed scoring a point.

'I see,' Debbie said, keeping her voice level. 'If he's really ill and they sent him home, it's possible that he collapsed on the way. We can check the hospitals –'

'There's nothing wrong with him,' Gary declared at once.

Debbie was surprised by the strength of his response. She gave a little smile. 'Well, there's no harm in checking, is there?'

Gary Burns was beginning to lose his cool. 'I don't know what the school are playing at,' he said hotly. 'They're meant to be responsible for the kids; you'd think they could manage that –'

'Let's find him first, eh?' Debbie said reassuringly. 'The best thing you can do is give us your number and go home. We'll contact you as soon as we know anything.'

Gary deliberately made his voice sound pleasant, but there was a nasty tone underlying it. 'Listen, love, I'm ten years older than you, so don't treat me like a kid. All right?'

Debbie deliberately did not react. 'If you can give me a description . . .'

In the CAD room, Polly Page was just reaching the end of a phone call. 'Thanks for letting us know, sir; we'll do what we can.' She cut the connection and turned to Sergeant Boyden.

'Sarge – that was Canley Comprehensive –'

Sergeant Boyden had been looking over Tony Stamp's shoulder, discussing a call, but he snapped to attention when Polly mentioned the school. 'Is this about Mike Burns?' he said, striding over to her workstation.

'Yes.' Polly sighed, expecting that the Sarge would find her information a bit of an anticlimax. 'His form teacher's worried. It seems the kids were expecting some kind of showdown between Mike Burns and Steve Rourke. That could be why Mike's gone missing.'

'So where's Steve Rourke?'

Polly sighed again. 'It seems he's gone missing as well. After Mike Burns's dad rang up, they checked: Steve's done a bunk.' She made a face. 'He plays truant all the time, so they hadn't really noticed before –'

Sergeant Boyden looked exasperated. 'So what on earth do they want us to do?'

'Find both of them, I suppose,' Polly said.

Sergeant Boyden gave a sigh of resignation. 'As if we hadn't got anything better to do . . .' He put on his headset and put out a call.

*

Reg answered and Boyden explained the position to him.

'George and I are going to check the Rourkes' flat,' Reg responded. 'We'll see if Steve's gone home.'

'Received, Reg.'

Reg clicked off the radio.

George moved the Panda out into the traffic. 'Some hope,' he snorted. 'You really think Steve Rourke's gone home and put his feet up after what's happened?'

'We've gotta give it a try,' Reg said, a little hurt.

'All units from Sierra Oscar,' Sergeant Boyden said. 'P1 Halpern Street and Brookvale Road. Ambulance on way. Informant's a Mrs Sue Kendall.'

WPC Norika Datta reached for her PR. 'Sierra Oscar from Sierra 85.'

'Go ahead, Norika,' Sergeant Boyden's voice said.

'Nick and I are in Old Seacoal Street,' Norika said. 'We'll deal with it, Sarge.'

'Received, Norika,' Boyden replied. 'The

40

victim's a pupil from Canley Comprehensive.'

In the CAD room, Polly turned around.
'Phew. It's all happening up there today.'
   'Yeah.' Boyden replied without thinking,
then he turned around, a grim expression on
his face. 'Maybe one of our missing persons
has just turned up.'

Meanwhile PC Nick Slater, in the car
with Norika, put on the blues and they
raced through the back roads to Halpern
Street.

Mrs Sue Kendall, the informant, was a smartly
dressed lady in her mid-thirties. She was
standing by the side of her car, which was
standing slewed across the junction with a
spiderweb of cracks across its windscreen. A
few yards away a bicycle lay on its side in the
road.
   'I've never had an accident before,' Mrs
Kendall said. She was speaking quickly, still
obviously shaken. 'I know everyone says that

but, honestly, I've never even had a parking ticket.'

'It's all right, Mrs Kendall,' Norika said, placing a hand gently on the woman's shoulder. 'No one's blaming you.'

Mrs Kendall had a pair of glasses in one hand; she kept putting them on and then taking them off. 'The car's just had its MOT,' she said. 'Look, wait, I'll show you.' She made a move to turn around and get into the car, but Norika stopped her. Behind her was the ambulance, where the paramedics were going about the calm but upsetting business of taking away an accident victim. Best to keep her away from that.

'Mrs Kendall, look, don't worry about that now.'

Mrs Kendall went back to putting her glasses on and taking them off again. Her voice shook slightly as she spoke again. 'Is he badly hurt?' She tried to glance behind her.

Norika moved slightly to one side to distract her attention. 'We don't know yet,' she said gently. 'Can you tell me what happened?'

'He just shot out of nowhere,' Mrs Kendall said.

'From where exactly?' Norika asked, looking at the layout of the surrounding roads.

Mrs Kendall turned and pointed. 'Down that hill – freewheeling. He was going really fast. I – I tried to swerve but he . . .'

Norika followed where the woman was indicating. The hill was long and steep, like a ski-run. Norika frowned. 'What, you mean he didn't use his brakes when he got to the road?'

Mrs Kendall spread her hands helplessly. 'Didn't even slow down.'

'Norika,' Nick called from behind her. He was standing by the car and the ambulance.

'That's it,' Mrs Kendall was saying. 'I don't understand.'

Norika touched her arm gently. 'Wait here,' she said quietly but firmly. 'I won't be a minute.' She moved away towards where the ambulance was waiting.

'Well it's not a fatac,' said Nick in a low voice. 'The boy's unconscious.'

Norika looked across at the stretcher. She

could see the red blanket with the strap round the lower legs in position. The boy's face was obscured by the green-suited paramedic who was fixing the top strap. 'What do they reckon?' Norika asked.

'Not good,' Nick replied. 'Head injuries.' Two paramedics wheeled the stretcher past them to the open door and slid it into the back of the ambulance. Norika got a clear view of the boy as they went past. It was only a brief glimpse but the details stayed with her: the head encased in bright plastic-coloured foam blocks to cushion it; the white plastic breathing-tube holding the boy's mouth open and his tongue down; the eyes closed and the face smeared with blood. The paramedics' precautionary measures made him look especially helpless.

There was another detail that Norika registered too. 'I know that boy,' she said. 'I've arrested him.' The ambulance pulled away.

Nick was nodding. He knew him too. 'Steve Rourke,' he said.

Six

CHERYL ROURKE COULD make out the silhouette of a black peaked cap through the oval of frosted glass in the front door. 'I don't believe this,' she said as she opened it. 'Three times in one day. Or have I won the lottery?'

'Er, Mrs Rourke, I'm PC Slater from Sun Hill. Can I have a word? It's about your son, Steve.' Nick looked past Cheryl into the flat.

Cheryl did not move from the doorstep. 'Go on, surprise me,' she said, taking a drag on a cigarette and leaning against the doorpost. 'What is it this time?'

Nick looked at her gravely.

A cold feeling ran down her spine. She

stepped back, her hand at the throat of her jumper; with her other hand she gestured to Nick to come in.

Inspector Andrew Monroe arrived at the scene of the accident. The ambulance had gone but Mrs Kendall's car was still there. Norika was waiting for him.

'The driver of the car said he came out of nowhere,' she said, leading the way under the blue-and-white tape labelled 'Police line – do not cross'. Their feet crunched on the fragments of glass that littered the road. 'Didn't even slow down. A lot of people say that, it's always the other vehicle; but I had a look, sir, I think she could be right.' She led him past the car and squatted down beside the twisted bicycle. 'The bike's a bit of a wreck, but look . . .' She leant down and reached for the end of a cable which was hanging loose. 'You can see the brakes have clearly been tampered with.'

Monroe leant forward to get a better view. 'Which would be consistent with a sidelong collision.'

'Yes, sir.' Monroe stood up and Norika followed suit.

'Nick's informed the next of kin,' she said. 'The boy hasn't come round. St Hugh's are going to phone through if he does.'

Monroe looked down at the bike and at the disconnected brake cable. 'So where was Steve earlier this morning?'

'Well, apparently Reg and George found him tied up and locked inside the pavilion on West Canley playing fields. They didn't pursue it because the boy didn't want to press charges.'

Monroe looked at her. 'And then he went to school?'

'Yeah. They saw him at the gate and he did register.'

Monroe began to walk back to his Panda. He reached the police line and looked around. They were finished now; some officers had arrived to lift the bike into the van and all the marks on the road had been catalogued and recorded. He pulled the tape away and crumpled it up into a sticky ball. Norika went to remove the other line.

Monroe had a sudden idea. He wandered over to Norika. 'Did Steve bike to school?'

'I can check that,' she replied. Her eyes and Monroe's met as they had the same thought. 'If he did . . .'

'Could be someone from there.' He opened his car door. 'The sooner we find Mike Burns the better.'

Norika was already hurrying away.

For the second time that day, Reg and George found themselves surrounded by the football memorabilia in Gary Burns's lounge. Gary was more nervous than he had been during that first visit.

Reg had his notebook out. 'Mr Burns,' he was saying, 'can you give us the names of any of Mike's friends?'

'Not really, no,' Gary Burns replied. 'He doesn't bring anyone round here.'

'Has he got a girlfriend?' George asked.

An ironic smile passed across Gary Burns's face. 'You must be joking.' He snorted. 'He's a bit of a late developer in that department.'

'Right,' George said, nodding. He wasn't surprised.

Reg said slowly: 'Are you sure you can't tell us where Mike might be?'

Gary Burns rolled his eyes to the ceiling. 'Look, if I knew, I wouldn't be asking you, would I? I mean you're the experts. He can't just disappear.'

'Look, Mr Burns,' George interrupted gently, 'it's vital that we talk to Mike. Now are you sure there's nothing you aren't telling us?'

Gary Burns spread his hands. 'Meaning what? You think I'm hiding him?'

'No,' George said smoothly, 'that's not what I'm suggesting.'

Mr Burns walked around to the mantelpiece and rested both hands on the wall above it, his head hanging down in an attitude of resignation. 'Look, there must be a million people with a grudge against the Rourke boy.' A hard note came into his voice. 'Why are you assuming it's down to Mike?'

'We aren't,' George said firmly. 'We don't

49

assume anything, that's why we need to talk to him.'

Gary Burns made no reply. After a short while Reg said: 'We think Mike's been having trouble from some of the other kids at school, Steve included.'

The man glanced around at the officers behind him. 'This is the first I've heard of it,' he said gruffly.

Reg continued, 'You said he doesn't go out much. Well, maybe he's afraid to. Steve is in a gang with the other boys and Mike is on his own.'

Gary Burns spoke to the wall. 'Mike can look after himself.'

Reg said patiently: 'Mr Burns, it's in both our interests to find your son, but it's difficult when we've got nothing to go on.'

Gary Burns didn't reply.

Reg was outside the record shop questioning two kids in school uniform. George was on the PR in the Panda. 'Sierra Oscar from 218.'

Polly Page's voice came through. 'Go ahead, George.'

'Yeah, we've checked the record shop on Dishman Street. Half of Canley Comprehensive's in there swapping CDs, but there's no sign of Mike Burns.'

'Received,' said Polly's voice.

George clicked off the PR. They had been to both nearby cafés, to the burger bar, the sports shop and all the newsagents in the area. Now they had just about run out of places to look.

Reg got in on the other side and belted up ready to leave. He had a thoughtful expression on his face. 'D'you know, I think we're approaching this all wrong.'

George put his belt on and looked wearily at Reg. 'Go on,' he said after a moment. 'Let's hear it.' He didn't sound at all hopeful that Reg would really have come up with anything, though.

Reg sighed. George was such a get-up-and-go type of copper that it was easy for him to misunderstand what someone less sure of themselves might do. 'Well,' he said, 'we're checking out all the places that kids go when they bunk off school, right? But they're places

51

where Steve and his mates are gonna be. Mike would stay well away.'

'Yes,' George said, his hand on the ignition key. 'So what's your idea?'

Reg shrugged. 'Well it's a school day, Mike's in school uniform. Anywhere outside of school, people are gonna notice him.'

George frowned deeply. 'What, so you reckon he's still in school?' He looked amazed.

Reg shrugged. 'Think about it. There are fourteen hundred kids in that school. The teachers don't even know all the ones they teach. They don't match names to faces. If Mike's not in lessons, they couldn't keep track of him.'

George began to see what Reg was getting at. He nodded slowly. 'We know he didn't go home . . .'

'Exactly,' Reg continued. 'Steve bunks off school as soon as he can. Mike knows that. The school's safe, it's the one place Steve won't be.'

Reg went to see Bill Wyatt. If anyone knew the kids' hiding-places, it was more likely to be him than a member of the teaching staff who had to maintain discipline. Sure enough, the caretaker led Reg to a little door at the end of the cloakroom and down some steps into the cellars, where the boiler-room was. There he put the light on, to reveal a long, stuffy, brickwork tunnel painted pale yellow and striped with pipes, some of them encased in dirty sponge material.

'Kids aren't meant to come down here,' Wyatt said, leading the way to the other end.

'But they do, though?' Reg said. Here and there tiny rooms led off on each side, and the whole tunnel was warm to the point of stuffiness. It was an ideal bolt-hole. He had a definite hunch about it.

Wyatt turned around and grinned briefly. 'They used to, whenever they fancied a quick cigarette. Regular smoker's corner, this. Then we put smoke alarms in, so now they use the bike sheds.' He stopped briefly to look into the boiler-room, but there was nobody in there.

'What about Mike?' Reg said. 'Where did he go?'

Wyatt gestured towards the end of the

corridor. It finished at a dead end, but then Reg saw that there was a door off to one side. 'There's my workshop. He comes and sits in there sometimes. He doesn't say much, keeps his head down. He hasn't been in there today, though.' Wyatt sighed and added in a lower voice: 'He's a nice lad, you know. No harm in him. Not a trouble-maker like some.'

Reg nodded.

A noise could be heard ahead of them: there was some scuffling, then something seemed to fall against something wooden. It made a loud clattering sound that nearly made Wyatt jump out of his skin.

Reg called out softly. 'Mike?' He moved over to the door that led off to the side.

When he looked inside he saw the boy, sprawled on the floor. He was trying to untangle himself from a pile of broken chairs that he had knocked over, some of which had fallen on him. When he heard Reg approach he stared at him, looking grimy and shaken, then he picked himself up.

Reg stepped back out into the corridor, and Mike followed uncertainly. When Wyatt saw him, he took a step backwards, a little awkward.

'Good guess, officer,' he said gravely. 'Well, I'll leave you to it.' He turned and walked away.

Reg turned back to the boy. 'Mike, what are you doing here? You know your father's reported you missing, don't you?'

'No,' Mike replied. He looked pale and resigned, as though he had thought he would be found for sure.

Reg thought that perhaps he had spoken a little too sharply. The poor kid looked miserable. 'Are you all right?' he asked.

'Yeah, I'm fine,' Mike said.

'But a teacher sent you home.'

'I wasn't ill,' Mike retorted hotly.

'He thought you were,' Reg insisted.

Mike looked down, embarrassed. 'I was sick in the bogs. Someone told the teacher; he said I should go home.'

Reg nodded towards Wyatt's workshop. 'Get your things.'

Mike already had his bag over one shoulder and he moved towards Reg reluctantly. They began to walk together back to the stairs.

'So why d'you come down here?' Reg asked.

Mike kept his head down. 'They was out to get me,' he mumbled miserably.

'Was Steve Rourke one of them?' Reg said.

The boy looked up immediately. 'What makes you say that?'

'Look,' Reg said evenly, 'Steve Rourke's been involved in an accident. He's badly hurt. His bike's gone into the side of a car. Looks as if someone's deliberately tampered with his bike. Now, if you're OK we need to talk to you down at the station.'

Mike's voice began to rise in panic. 'Are you arresting me?'

They had reached the bottom of the stairs. Reg took the boy by the elbow to steer him upwards. 'We can't talk to you on your own,' he said, 'so your father will have to sit in on any interview.'

Mike looked back at him. He seemed baffled and horrified. 'You are arresting me, aren't you?'

Seven

THE TWIN TAPES in the interview-room cassette recorder were turning slowly. Inspector Monroe sat next to the black square microphone mounted on the wall, facing Mike Burns across the table. With Mike was his father. Reg Hollis was seated by Inspector Monroe's side. He checked that the recorder was working properly as Monroe began the interview.

'You were found on the school premises at one forty-five?' Monroe said gently. He was a big man, tough and energetic, and usually put the fear of God into everyone. Reg was impressed, though, with how carefully he was treading with Mike, how he was trying to put the boy at ease.

Gary Burns's eyes darted from Monroe to Mike. He looked keyed-up, but less keyed-up than his son.

'Yeah,' Mike answered in a monotone.

'How long had you been there?'

'Dunno,' Mike said. He stared at the table. 'Hours.'

'Did you go anywhere else in school?' Monroe said.

'Registration.'

'Did you go to the bike sheds?' Monroe asked.

Gary Burns stiffened.

'No,' Mike said.

Gary Burns let out a sharp sigh like steam escaping from a kettle. 'You don't have to answer,' he said to his son. 'You can just say "No comment."'

Monroe looked at Gary. 'Please don't interrupt,' he said shortly. He turned back to Mike. 'You told PC Hollis that you were afraid some other boys in the school were going to beat you up.'

'Yeah,' Mike said, then he glanced to one side. Gary Burns was watching him closely.

Monroe added carefully: 'And Steve Rourke was one of the people threatening you.'

Gary Burns's eyes snapped from Mike to Monroe. 'Wait a minute, you can't ask him that.'

'Yes, I can,' Monroe replied calmly. He looked at Mike again, and he kept his voice gentle. 'Had Steve or his friends beaten you up before?'

Mike was still looking at the table. 'No, but . . .' He made a noise as though he was going to add something, but then said, 'No.'

Monroe looked closely at him as though by doing so he could get the boy to raise his head. 'Well, why did you think they would today?'

Mike looked at his father and then at Monroe. 'I don't know why.'

Monroe looked at him earnestly, trying to will the boy into establishing eye-contact. 'Had they been bullying you before today?'

Mike hesitated, and Gary leant across and put his hand on the table between Monroe and his son. 'No comment,' he said quickly.

Mike glanced at him, a sick look in his eyes.

Monroe looked at Gary. 'Mr Burns,' he said firmly, 'I'm asking your son.'

Gary Burns looked pointedly at Mike. 'You don't have to say anything, Mike. You don't have to say anything at all.'

Mike looked at Monroe uncertainly. Very gently, Monroe repeated the question. 'Mike, had they been bullying you before?'

Mike continued looking at the floor. 'Yeah.'

'So what did you want to do?' Monroe asked next.

A flicker of discomfort passed over Mike's face. 'It's OK,' Monroe added. 'Take your time.'

Gary Burns watched tensely.

'I just wanted to stay out of their way,' Mike said.

'And what happened?' Monroe asked.

Gary slapped his hand down hard on the table. 'I want to stop this interview,' he said, angrily. 'I think we should get a solicitor.' His eyes glared a challenge at Monroe and Reg.

Mike stared at his father. He looked very upset. 'You think I did it?'

'Just shut up, will you?' Gary Burns replied irritably.

Something snapped inside Mike. He pushed back the chair and stood up. His fists were tight, the knuckles white with rage. He yelled at the man, 'Stop telling me what to do!'

Reg said quietly: 'For the benefit of the tape, Mike has just stood up.'

'Mike, sit down, please,' Monroe said calmly.

Mike Burns stayed on his feet. He looked at Reg and Monroe, his anger already subsiding into a look of sick helplessness: he was at the end of his tether. 'Look, I want to talk to you alone.' He leant back against the wall and avoided his father's gaze.

Monroe said evenly: 'As we explained earlier, you have to be interviewed in the presence of an appropriate adult.' He looked from Mike to Gary Burns, then added casually: 'Of course that doesn't have to be a member of your family.'

Gary was immediately appalled. 'Now wait a minute . . .' he began.

Monroe said matter-of-factly: 'It could be a social worker.'

'He doesn't need a social worker!' Gary Burns shouted angrily. He stared at Monroe.

'Or,' Monroe went on, 'any responsible adult over the age of eighteen not connected with the police.'

'I want to talk to someone else,' Mike demanded, his eyes looking straight at Monroe and avoiding Gary. It seemed as though he was scared of him. 'Not – not a lawyer . . .' he said hesitantly. 'Just someone else.'

Monroe looked at his watch. 'Interview terminated at fourteen ten.'

Reg switched off the tape.

Monroe raised his head. 'Who would you like?' he said to Mike.

'It doesn't matter,' Mike said bitterly. He gave a nervous gesture. 'Anyone.'

Gary Burns was staring at his son in disbelief. 'What are you doing?' he demanded, then he made an effort to control the anger in his voice. 'Mike,' he tried to sound kind, 'come on.'

'Mr Burns,' Monroe said firmly, 'Mike has the right . . .'

Gary waved him away. 'Never mind that,' he snapped. He turned back to Mike, his patience shattered. 'I want a straight answer,' he said firmly. 'What are you playing at?'

Mike yelled back at him, 'Standing up for myself.' He gave a tiny smile. 'Just like you told me.'

Eight

NICK SLATER AND Norika Datta had driven Cheryl Rourke to St Hugh's Hospital. Nick dropped them off and Norika accompanied Mrs Rourke into the casualty area. As they made enquiries at the front desk, a doctor pushed through some swing doors and came towards them.

'Are you Steven Rourke's next of kin?' The doctor wore a white coat over a surgical gown and looked pale and drawn; as if she had been up for most of the night.

Cheryl Rourke put her hand to her throat. She tried to speak but suddenly couldn't.

'That's right,' Norika said. 'This is his mother.'

The doctor looked at Cheryl. 'We've been trying to contact you, Mrs Rourke. We've taken your son into surgery; he had some pressure on the brain.'

Cheryl gasped and swayed. Norika put a hand on her arm to steady her.

'Are you all right, Mrs Rourke?' she asked gently. 'Is there a friend or neighbour you would like us to fetch?'

Cheryl wasn't paying any attention to her. She took a deep breath and said to the doctor: 'What do you mean, pressure on the brain?'

The doctor sighed, and gave Cheryl a look of weary compassion. 'It's quite a routine thing in these circumstances, Mrs Rourke. You can wait for him . . .'

Norika wondered how long the doctor had been on duty. It was as if her exhaustion had made her forget that she was dealing with life and death and not with broken machines on a conveyor belt.

Cheryl rapped out another question. 'Where is he now?'

'He's in theatre six,' the doctor replied.

'How long will he be in there?' Cheryl asked hoarsely.

'It's hard to say; four hours, maybe. Could be as long as eight.'

Norika took her arm gently. 'Come on, Mrs Rourke; I know a place where you will be more comfortable.' She looked at the doctor. 'It's all right, I know my way.'

The doctor nodded to her and walked away to the casualty desk to pick up a clipboard.

Norika led Cheryl away to the lift, and then through tiled corridors painted in a shade of green that must have been intended to be restful, but which merely made the place more unfriendly. They followed the signs marked 'Head injuries'. People bustled past them in and out of swing doors which occasionally gave glimpses of machinery or pale-looking people propped up on stark white pillows.

As they were walking, Cheryl put her hand in her bag and took out a packet of Marlboro cigarettes. With her other hand she attempted to light a match, but her hands were so unsteady that she couldn't.

Norika watched her make a few attempts then gently took the match out of her hand.

Cheryl swore at her. 'You mean I can't have a fag? My son's lying in there and –'

'There's a smoking room by the head injuries unit,' Norika told her.

At last they came to the head injuries unit. Norika led Cheryl to the smoking room and lit a cigarette for her, then went back out to the duty nurse to make some enquiries.

Steve was still in theatre.

Norika turned to go back to Cheryl to give her the news and to ask her again if she wanted to contact a friend.

Suddenly the swing doors at the end of the corridor were pushed open roughly and half a dozen kids in Canley Comprehensive uniforms pushed through. Talking loudly and angrily, they jostled their way past Norika, nearly knocking her over, and went up to the duty nurse's desk.

A tall youth who was wearing big air-pumped trainers demanded: 'Can we see Steve Rourke?'

'I'm sorry,' the nurse said, 'but that's not

possible. Are you next of kin? How did you get this far?'

'We're his mates,' another youth protested.

'You're not actually relatives?'

There was a lot of noise as each one began to speak at once. The nurse stood up and tried to raise her voice above it. Norika heard her say: 'If you're going to stay here, you'll have to wait over there quietly.' She pointed to a row of seats. The youths quietened down and crossed, grumbling, to the row of seats opposite the desk. The nurse cast a worried look in Norika's direction. The WPC gave her a reassuring smile and said: 'Just let them sit quietly.' The nurse, still looking anxious, went back to her paperwork.

Norika went through to the smoking room to give Cheryl the news about Steve. While she was doing so, she heard a commotion in the corridor outside, then the door to the smoking room was pushed open. A pair of Canley boys came in, one defiantly lighting a cigarette and passing it to the other, who sucked on it hurriedly.

They crossed the room and sat down at the

other side, sharing the cigarette in silence as though they didn't quite dare hold a conversation. They kept looking at Norika.

Eventually she went over to them. 'Is there something you want to tell me?'

The taller one avoided her gaze and muttered something to the other one. His companion said: 'Have you found Mike Burns yet?'

'Why d'you want to know?' Norika replied.

The boy turned to look out of the window and sucked on the last of the cigarette. He stubbed it out viciously. 'Make sure you string him up.'

Monroe took Gary Burns to the front interview room to calm him down – and to keep him away from Mike.

Gary would rather have paced around instead of sitting down, but he regained his composure quite quickly.

'Look,' he said with a smile that was intended to be an apology, 'I was totally out of order in there, OK? I'm sorry.' He was the kind of man who made apologizing to someone sound as if he were doing them a big favour. He went on, confidently: 'I'd like to have a word with Mike, sort things out.'

He obviously did not feel he really needed the inspector's permission so it gave Monroe a certain amount of pleasure to say politely: 'I'm afraid that's impossible until we've finished interviewing him.'

Like anyone who has just discovered that he cannot use a little charm to bend the rules, Gary was instantly angry. 'Bullied him into confessing more like,' he retorted.

Monroe replied: 'It's not our intention to bully Mike into anything. He doesn't want you present at the interview; that's his choice.'

'This is ridiculous,' Gary protested. 'I'm his dad.'

Monroe said evenly: 'Well, maybe he feels he can't talk in front of you.'

'But I haven't done anything,' Gary said. 'I mean, all I did was tell him to pull himself together.'

Monroe's eyes narrowed and he looked at Gary Burns carefully. 'When was this?' he asked.

'Today,' Gary said, then he paused, embarrassed. When he went on, some of the wind had been taken out of his sails. 'Some of the kids have been giving him a hard time. I told him to stand up for himself and stop taking it lying down. It was time to sort things out once and for all.'

Monroe said quietly: 'Looks as if he's taken your advice, doesn't it?'

Nine

MIKE CHOSE BILL Wyatt as the adult to accompany him in his interview. Monroe was able to continue the interview at three fifteen. Reg was operating the tape as before. Mike sat sideways on the chair with his back against the wall, and he spent most of the time looking down, but he seemed less tense. Monroe kept his approach gentle, but he thought the boy was almost relieved to be able to talk at last.

'When I was in the football team,' Mike said, 'Steve made everyone go for me, behind Dad's back. Dad never saw. So I quit. From then on Steve was out to get me.'

Monroe said: 'You never told your father?'

Mike rolled his eyes. 'You're joking,' he said with a snort of bitter laughter. 'Steve's one of Dad's star players. He wanted me to be like him.'

'How long's this gone on?' Monroe asked.

'A year,' Mike replied. He shrugged, and a hard edge came into his voice. 'One more year and I can leave.'

'So what happened this morning?' Monroe asked slowly.

Mike looked at the floor in silence. 'Steve trashed my bike yesterday. I went to get it; it was wrecked. He was there, he just smiled, like, "What you gonna do?"'

Reg winced.

Mike continued: 'I went home. Dad was going to football practice.' He stopped, uncertain.

Monroe prompted him. 'And you told him?'

Mike looked up in anguish. 'He made me. Those bikes are really pricey. I told him all about Steve. He went mental –' Mike stopped again.

'Go on,' Monroe prompted him.

Mike's face twisted in a mixture of misery and pain. He spoke quickly, each memory reminding him of the unfairness of it all. 'This morning he had a go at me, said it was my fault. I should stand up to people, sort things out. He said he was ashamed of me.'

'What did you do?' Monroe asked.

Mike bit his lip. 'I went to school. Steve was there, he said that was it, after school he'd be waiting for me . . .' He broke off abruptly. 'Is he going to die?'

Wyatt looked away, as if he thought that perhaps he shouldn't be witnessing some of this. But he stayed quiet.

'We don't know,' Monroe said. He looked at the boy earnestly. 'Mike, if you know anything, you should tell us.'

There was a short period of silence. Mike swallowed, then said: 'He trashed my bike, I trashed his.'

Monroe kept his voice even. 'What did you do exactly?'

'The brakes,' Mike said flatly. He was staring at the floor. 'It's easy, just loosen the cables and . . .'

Out of the corner of his eye Monroe saw Wyatt give an involuntary start. He spoke quickly to Mike in case the man's reaction should distract Mike from his story. 'When was this?'

'Registration.' Again his voice was flat, as if he was relating something that had happened to someone else, or something he had not yet come to terms with. 'I had to do it then. Steve's always registered. Then he bunks off, usually at breaktime.'

'What did you do then?' Monroe asked.

'I –' Mike began to speak but then he caught his breath, as if what he was about to say was embarrassing. 'I was sick,' he said in a quiet voice. 'Mr Godwin said to go home. I wanted to go back but I couldn't, see? Steve was waiting.'

'So you went and hid?' Monroe suggested.

'I couldn't go home,' Mike repeated. 'Dad would have –' He tailed off and shrugged. 'It was stupid,' he mumbled.

'Well, not very sensible,' Monroe agreed gently.

Mike's head snapped up and he looked at

75

the inspector as if the man hadn't understood a word of it. 'You don't get it, do you? This'll make things worse.' He looked away into the corner of the room and carried on, bitterly: 'I should've had a fight with Steve, done it properly.'

Wyatt started; he was shocked to see how upset the boy was becoming.

Reg caught his eye and tried to give him an understanding look. Being the 'appropriate adult' was often quite upsetting.

Mike thumped his clenched fist down on the table. 'I should have punched his lights out.'

'You think that would have settled it?' Monroe asked him.

'It's what Dad would do,' the boy answered. 'It works for him, doesn't it? He doesn't get any trouble from anyone.'

Monroe took a deep breath, thinking. Then he said: 'From what you're saying, today Steve was out to get you. Do you know why?'

'It's what they're like,' Mike said shortly.

'Not according to what you've said,' Monroe replied, speaking quietly but firmly.

'He and his friends hadn't beaten you up before, but they were going to today. Why?'

Mike shook his head. 'I don't know.'

'Last night,' Monroe said, 'someone, we don't know who, tied Steve up and locked him in the pavilion.'

'I wasn't there, was I?' Mike snapped.

'This morning,' Monroe went on, 'Steve was out to get you.' He lowered his head to try to make some eye-contact with Mike. 'D'you see what I'm asking?'

'I told you what I did,' Mike said miserably.

'Mike,' Monroe said in the same calm but firm tone, 'I'm going to ask you something. I want you to think about it carefully. Did you or your father have anything to do with what happened to Steve yesterday?'

Mike stared at the floor but did not answer.

'All right,' Monroe said. He tried a different approach. 'Do you know who locks up after football practice?'

Mike shrugged.

There was silence.

After a moment, Wyatt answered the question. 'Gary Burns locks the place up, then he gets the keys back to me.' He looked steadily at Monroe.

Reg whistled softly. Monroe looked from Wyatt to Reg for a moment without speaking. Then he looked at Mike. 'Mike, did your father lock Steve up as a punishment? Is that why Steve was out to get you?'

'No comment,' said Mike, and turned away. They couldn't see his face.

Monroe tried to push further. 'Mike –' he began.

Mike looked up at him. 'No comment,' he repeated, and he turned his gaze away to the other end of the room.

Monroe persisted. 'Mike, we have to know what's happened.' He paused, then said again: '*Everything* that's happened.'

Mike looked up at him again. 'Why?' he said savagely. 'You're not going to help me, are you?' He glanced at Wyatt and then at Monroe. 'I've got nothing else to say.'

Ten

MONROE CAME OUT to the front inter-view room where Gary Burns had been waiting. It was now four o'clock and the man had had plenty of time on his own to think about what might be going on in the interview. When he saw Monroe, he stood up quickly. Even before Monroe had closed the door he took a breath to speak, but then he tried to hide his agitation by sounding casual.

'Simple question: I want to know what Mike's been charged with.' He gave a smile that was supposed to look confident.

Monroe studied the man's discomfort and thought he probably deserved every second of it. However, he replied: 'It's not possible to say at the moment. The case papers'll go to YACS – that's the Youth and Community Section – and they'll have to look at the whole situation.' He watched Gary Burns gravely and then added: 'Could be GBH with intent of anything up to murder.'

Gary could not believe his ears. 'You mean he's gonna get locked up?'

'He's free to go for the moment. If the Rourke boy dies, then obviously that could change.'

Gary Burns paced up to the wall, dragging his fingers through his hair. 'Steve Rourke started all of this,' he said roughly. 'If it hadn't been for him . . .'

Monroe looked at him, his expression hardening. 'And you tied him up. Locked him up as a punishment.'

Gary Burns froze, startled. He turned slowly and looked at Monroe. 'Mike told you?'

Monroe shook his head. He said quietly: 'No, Mike wouldn't tell us.' He looked at Gary gravely, a challenge in his eyes. 'That's what you did, though, isn't it?'

Gary was genuinely flustered. For a moment all he could do was breathe deeply, then eventually he said defensively: 'I wanted a bit of respect. He was totally out of line.'

Monroe folded his arms and leant back against the door. 'So what exactly were you planning to do?'

Gary began to pace again. 'Give him some time to think about it. I thought a night in the cold would wipe the smirk off his face.' He shrugged and looked at Monroe. Again the smile, only this time with a little more confidence. 'Anyway, who cares, he's not bringing charges.'

Monroe remained unmoved. 'If he does recover, I personally will do everything in my power to make him change his mind.'

'You can try,' Gary retorted immediately, his voice rising, 'but it's not a police matter.' He made a fist of one hand and thumped it against the flat of the other. 'Steve knows that. It's between him and me.' He glared at Monroe.

Monroe shook his head slowly. 'It's a shame

Mike's the one who's being punished then, isn't it?'

Gary Burns rounded on him, outraged. 'I did this for Mike!'

'And it never occurred to you that if you picked on Steve, Steve would take it out on your son.' Monroe shook his head again. He did not bother to hide his disgust. 'You set Mike up, whether you meant to or not. If the Rourke boy dies, your son could be charged with murder; and that's a whole different ballgame.'

Gary looked appalled. 'The press would crucify me,' he exclaimed.

Monroe stared at him with barely disguised loathing. 'And that's all you care about?' he said quietly.

The ex-professional footballer looked away. Monroe thought he detected a trace of shame on the man's face – at last.

'So what happens now?' Gary Burns asked bitterly. It was as though he was grudgingly accepting the situation for the first time.

A hard edge crept into Monroe's voice. 'For the moment we're releasing Mike into your care because we've no other choice.' He reached for the door handle. 'You can explain it all to him.'

Gary Burns followed Monroe out to the front entrance. Mike was already there, looking tired and bewildered. Beside him was Reg, with an interview tape and a custody sheet.

Reg saw Gary glance at the tape and then look extremely cross. Reg knew that look. It said: how did things ever get so far that the police were dragged in? Gary would probably give his eye-teeth to know what was on that tape.

Gary Burns stopped near Mike, but he did not go very close to the boy. He seemed to be wary of him, keeping his distance. 'All right?' he asked.

Mike did not answer or look at him.

Gary nodded towards the door. 'The car's parked out front.' He smiled.

Mike turned and walked towards the door, fast. Gary called his name uncertainly and hurried after him. He caught up with the boy and put a hand on his arm. Mike shook it off angrily and shoved his way out through the glass doors.

Reg and Monroe watched as Gary Burns stopped and composed himself, then he followed Mike out and down the steps.

'It's always the quiet ones, Reg,' Monroe said.

POLICE TERMS

Alco	Anything to do with the breath test for drivers
AMIP	Area Major Incident Pool
ARPO	Area Press and Publicity Officer
ARB	Accident Report Book
ARV	Armed Response Vehicle
Big House	Crown Court
Black Rat	Traffic Patrol Officer
Blag	Robbery
Blagger	Robber
A body	An arrest
Brains Dept	CID (used by uniformed officers)
Button Mob	Uniformed officers (used by CID)
CAD	Computer Aided Despatch
CID	Criminal Investigation Department
Civvies	Civilian support staff
CLO	Community Liaison Officer

CSG	Crime Support Group
Corres	Correspondence, paperwork
DC	Detective Constable
DCI	Deputy Chief Inspector
DCO	Divisional Community Officer
Dipper	Pickpocket
Drum	House
Esso	Every Saturday and Sunday off (a good shift)
Factory	Police Station
Fatac	Fatal accident
Fence	Person who sells on stolen goods
FME	Force Medical Examiner
GBH	Grievous Bodily Harm
Going up the road	Committed to the Crown Court
GP	General Purpose vehicle (usually unmarked car)
Handling	Handling stolen goods
Have it on your toes	Run away

IC1, 2, 3, etc.	Identity Codes describing race of a suspect
IR	Information Room
IRB	Incident Room Book
Middle of the yarder	Confidential conversation
MS15	Complaints Investigation
MSS	Message Switching System
NCPA	No Cause for Police Action
NDIU	National Drugs Intelligence Unit
NFA	No Further Action
NIB	National Identification Bureau
Nondy	Nondescript, unmarked car
NSY	New Scotland Yard
OB	Occurrence Book
Obbo	Observation
OP	Observation Point
Oppo	Mate, partner
OTS	Over the side
Pars	Particulars of an occurrence

PC	Police Constable
Plonks	Women PCs
PNC	Police National Computer
Polac	Police accident
PR	Personal radio
Put on the blues	Turn on the siren and flashing light
Run in	Yard housing stolen goods or vehicles
Sarge	Sergeant
Skip	Sergeant
SOCO	Scenes of Crimes Officer
SO5	Index of Missing Persons
SO8	Robbery Squad
SO9	Regional Crime Squad
SO19	Firearms Unit
Spin	Search
TD	Traffic Officer
TI	Trainee Investigator
TSG	Territorial Support Group
VDU	Visual Display Unit, computer screen
W	Warrant
Wheels	Motor Vehicle

Woodentops	Uniformed officers (used by CID)
YACS	Youth and Community Section
The Yard	New Scotland Yard

CALL SIGNS

A Alpha	N November
B Bravo	O Oscar
C Charlie	P Papa
D Delta	Q Quebec
E Echo	R Romeo
F Foxtrot	S Sierra
G Golf	T Tango
H Hotel	U Uniform
I India	V Victor
J Juliet	W Whisky
K Kilo	X X-Ray
L Lima	Y Yankee
M Mike	Z Zulu

Sun Hill is known as 'S' Division, so all its IDs begin with Sierra:

Sierra Oscar	Sun Hill
Sierra 1	Area Car
Sierra Oscar 1	Duty Officer
Sierra Oscar 2	Station van
Sierra Oscar 3	Section Sergeant

Sierra Oscar 4	Uniformed officers
Sierra Oscar 5	CID
Sierra Oscar 6	CID
Sierra Oscar 7	CID
Sierra Oscar 8	CID
Sierra Oscar 51	Chief Superintendent
Sierra Oscar 54	Chief Inspector
Sierra Oscar 56	Detective Chief Inspector
Sierra Oscar 84, etc.	Panda cars